GOT LEGENDS ALPHABET

Words by Robin Feiner

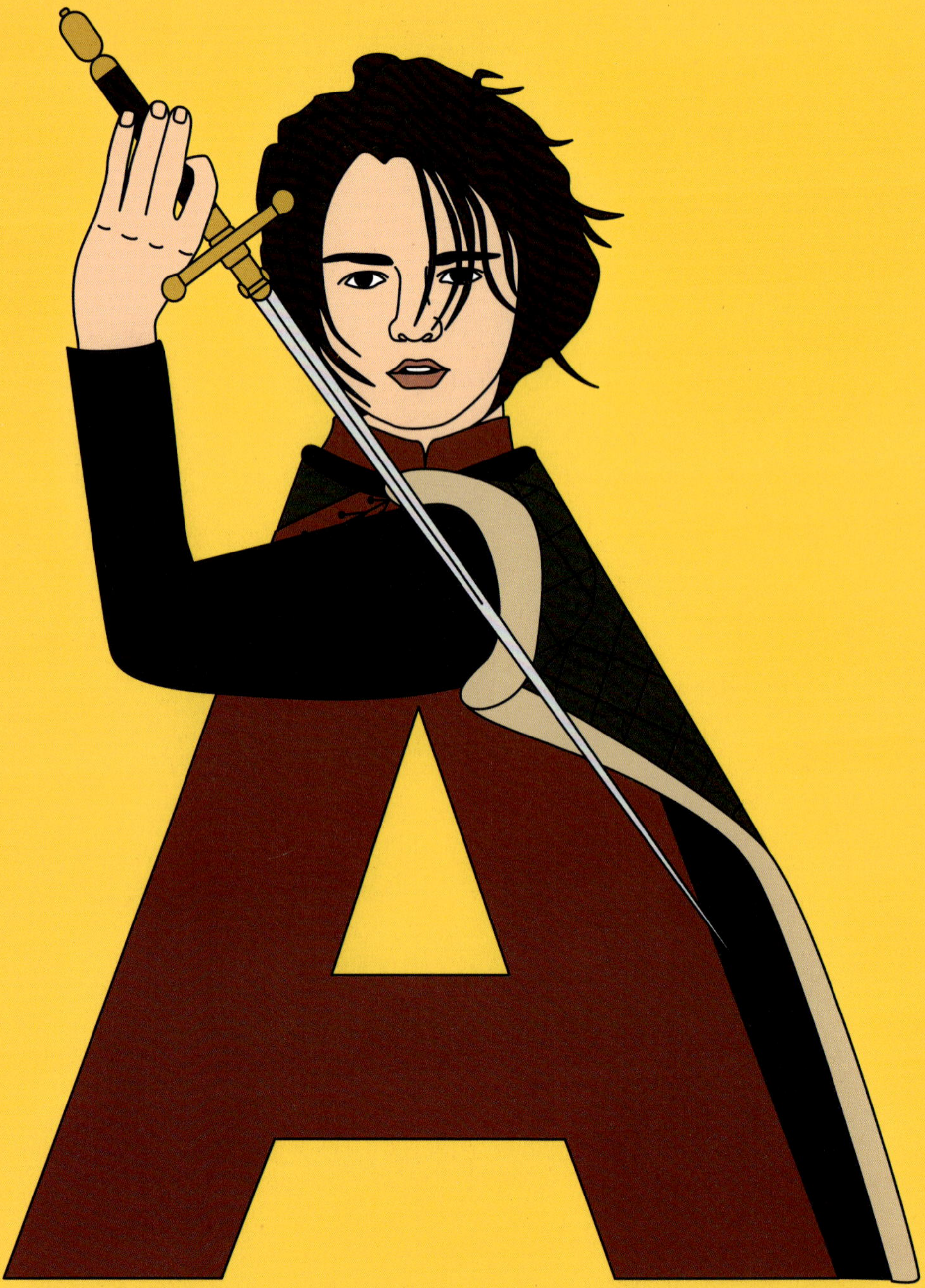

Aa

A is for **A**rya Stark. Stay off this legend's list. Often overlooked, Arya uses her trusty Needle and lessons from Jon Snow, Syrio Forel, the Hound, and the Faceless Men to become one of the toughest fighters in the realm. Just ask the Night King and House Frey.

Bb

B is for **B**ran Stark. Bad luck landed young Brandon in a wheelchair. But magical warg and greensight powers allow this legend to stand tall and fly high above the realm as the Three-Eyed Raven before becoming the ruler of the Six Kingdoms.

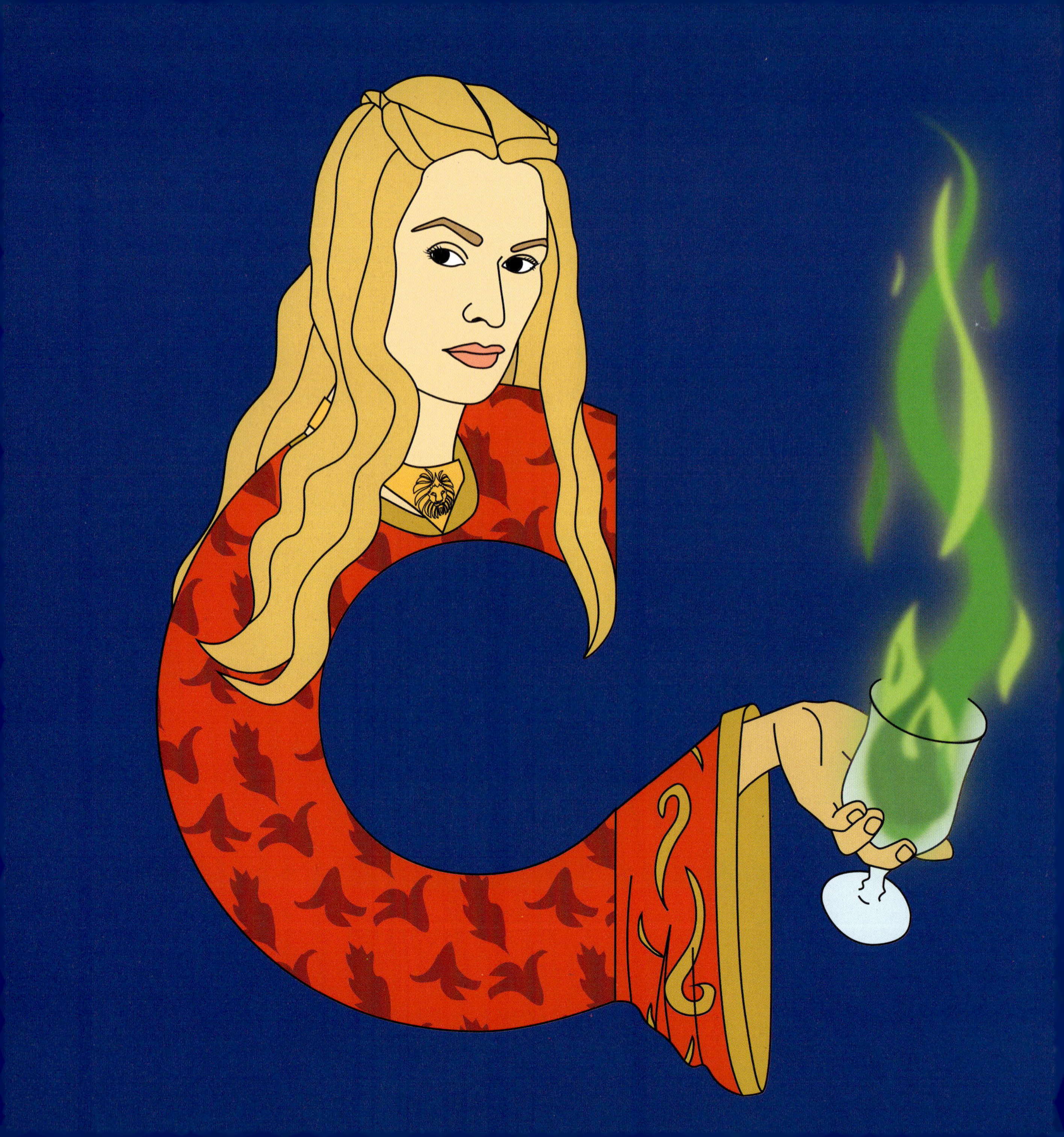

Cc

C is for **C**ersei Lannister. This queen will do anything for those she loves. Never afraid to choose violence, Cersei and her legendary thirst for vengeance are almost unmatched. From her own husband to her worst enemies, Cersei will stop at nothing, no matter the cost. Shame! Shame! Shame!

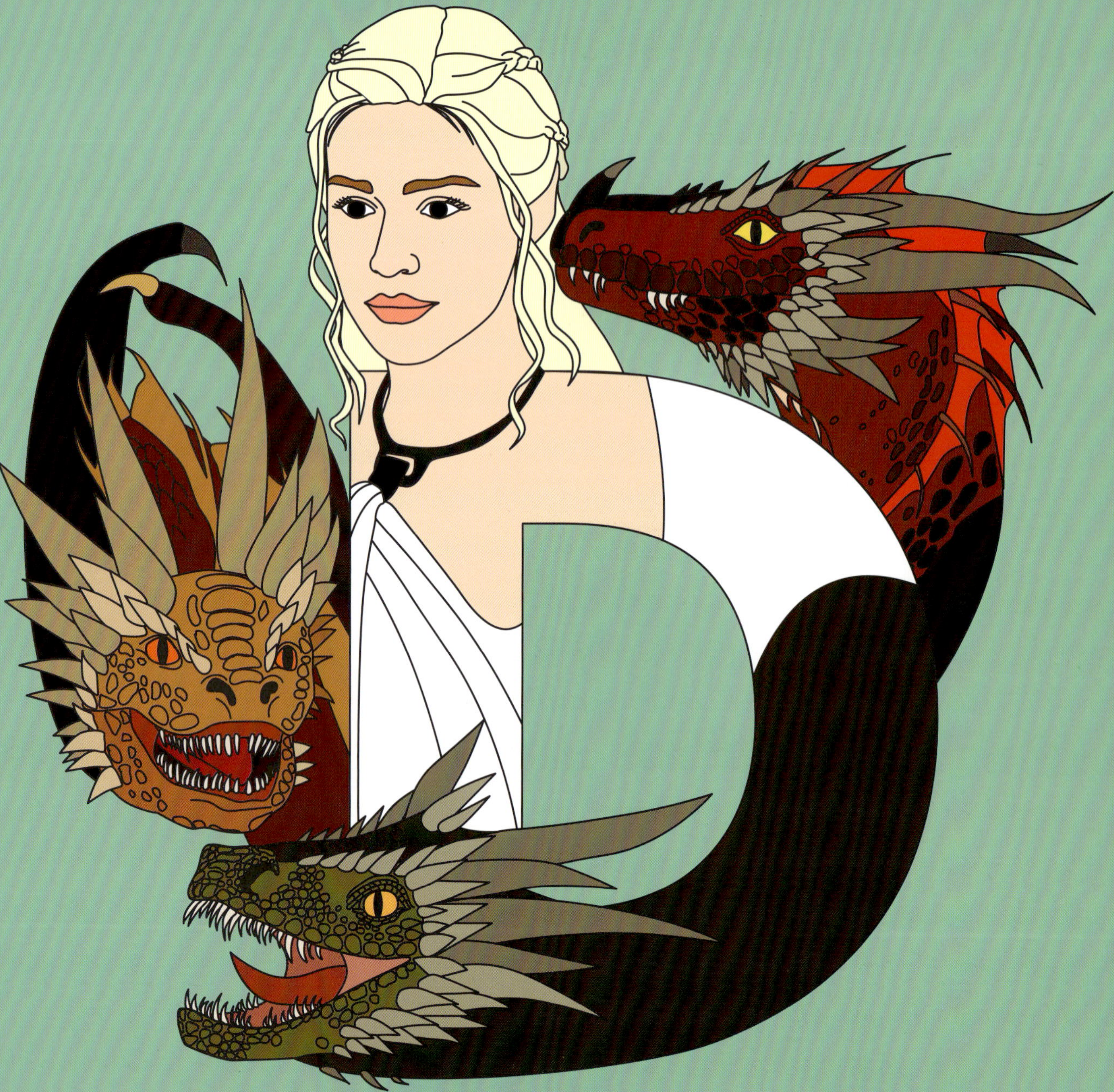

Dd

D is for **D**aenerys Targaryen (and Her Dragons). Daenerys Stormborn, the Mother of Dragons, the Breaker of Chains—Dany is a legend by any name. With the help of Drogon, Rhaegal, and Viserion, Dany ascends to dizzying heights in the realm before her madness gets the best of her.

E

Ee

E is for Eddard Stark. Better known as Ned, this man has a sense of honor that is nothing short of legendary. As a father, head of House Stark, and Hand of the King, Ned always does what he thinks is right. Unfortunately, such loyalty to truth and justice can cause men to lose their heads.

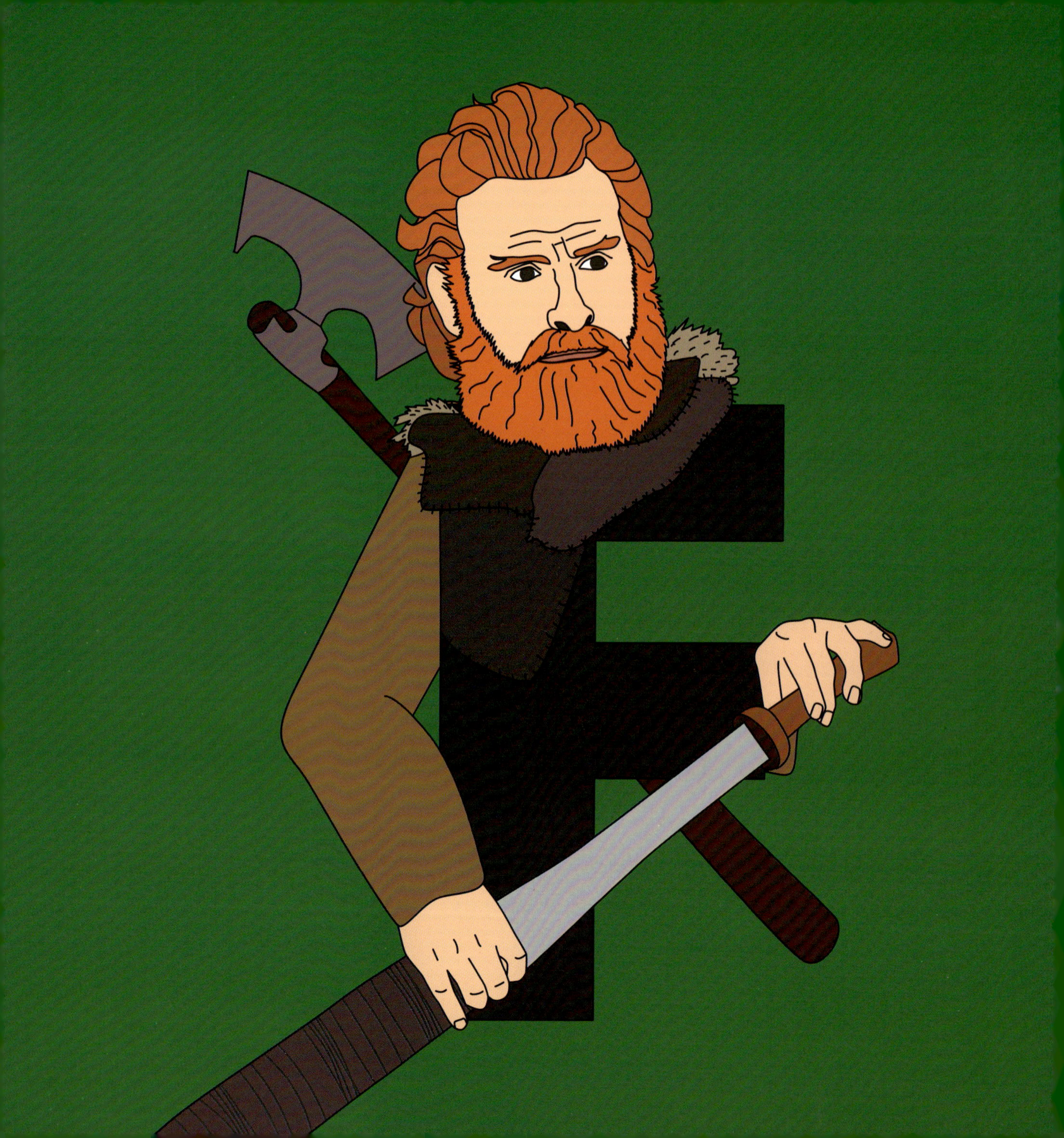

Ff

F is for **F**ree Folk. These wildlings live north of the Wall, free of the laws of the Seven Kingdoms. Many think Free Folk are nothing but untamable beasts. But those same people have legends such as Tormund Wolfsbane to thank for their lives.

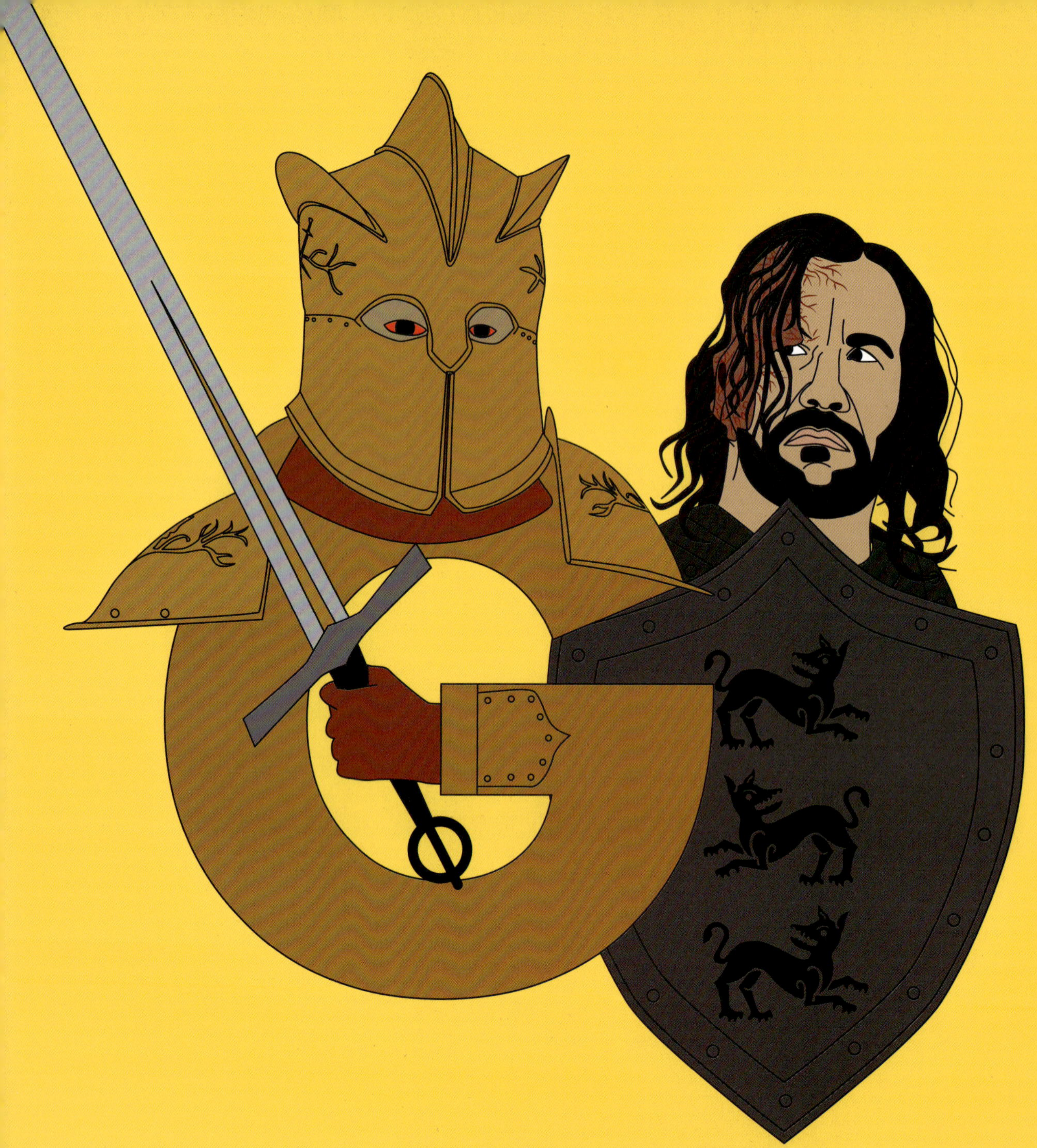

Gg

G is for **G**regor Clegane. Strap in for Cleganebowl. Freakishly big and freakishly strong, the 'Mountain' is legendary for his brutality and temper. Former knight Gregor is brought back from near death to become nearly unstoppable. That is, until he goes head-to-head with the 'Hound,' his younger brother Sandor.

H

Hh

H is for **H**odor.
Hold the door! This loyal legend was once a nice young boy named Wylis, but after a seizure, he became a simple-minded servant of the Stark family. Big, strong, and kind-hearted, Hodor serves the Starks until the bitter end. Hodor!

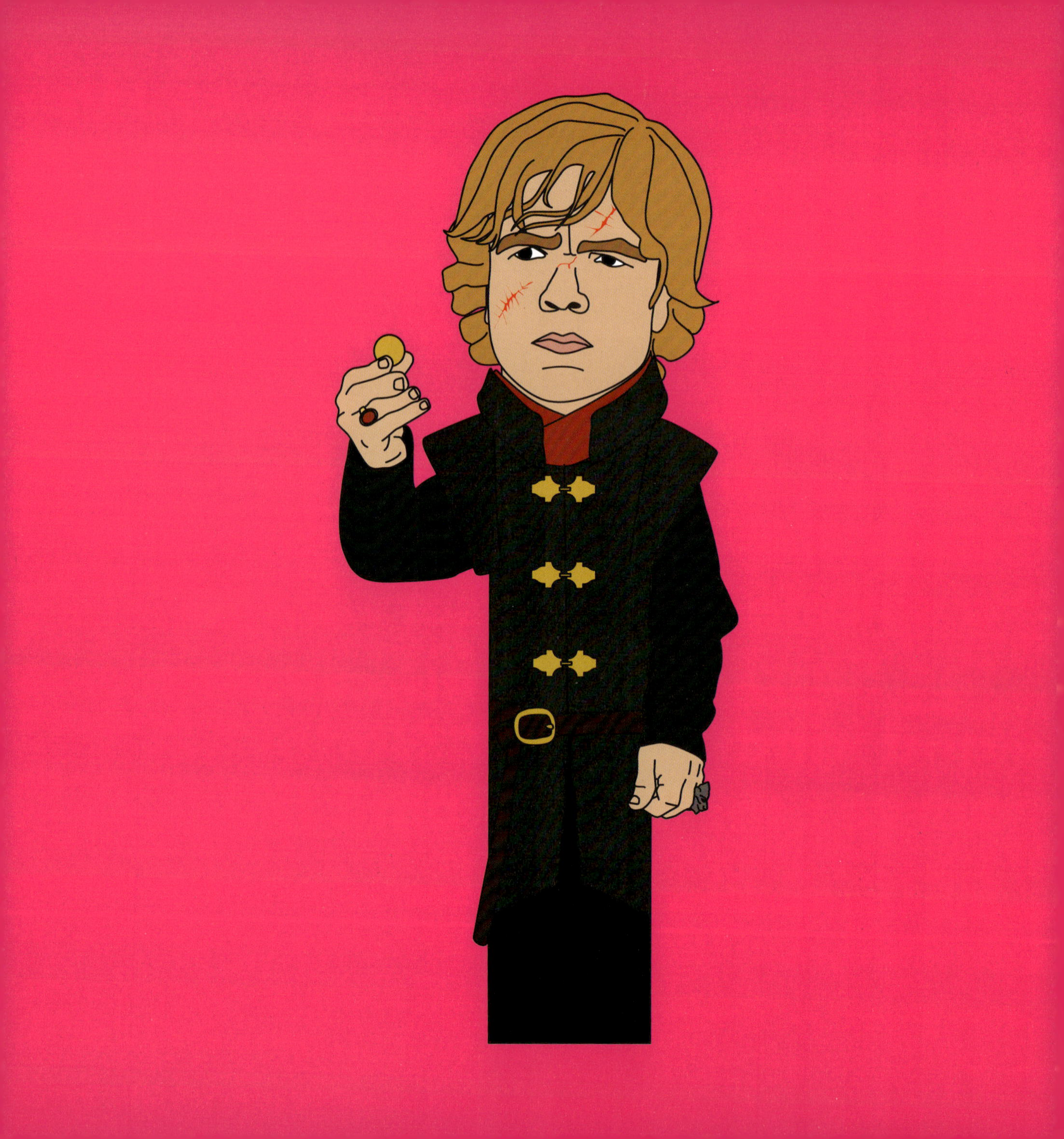

Ii

I is for the 'Imp'.
Tyrion Lannister drinks, and he knows things. A Lannister always pays their debts, and the man many call the Imp owes plenty to his enemies. From taking out father Tywin to the Battle of the Blackwater, this legend knows how to win and have a good time.

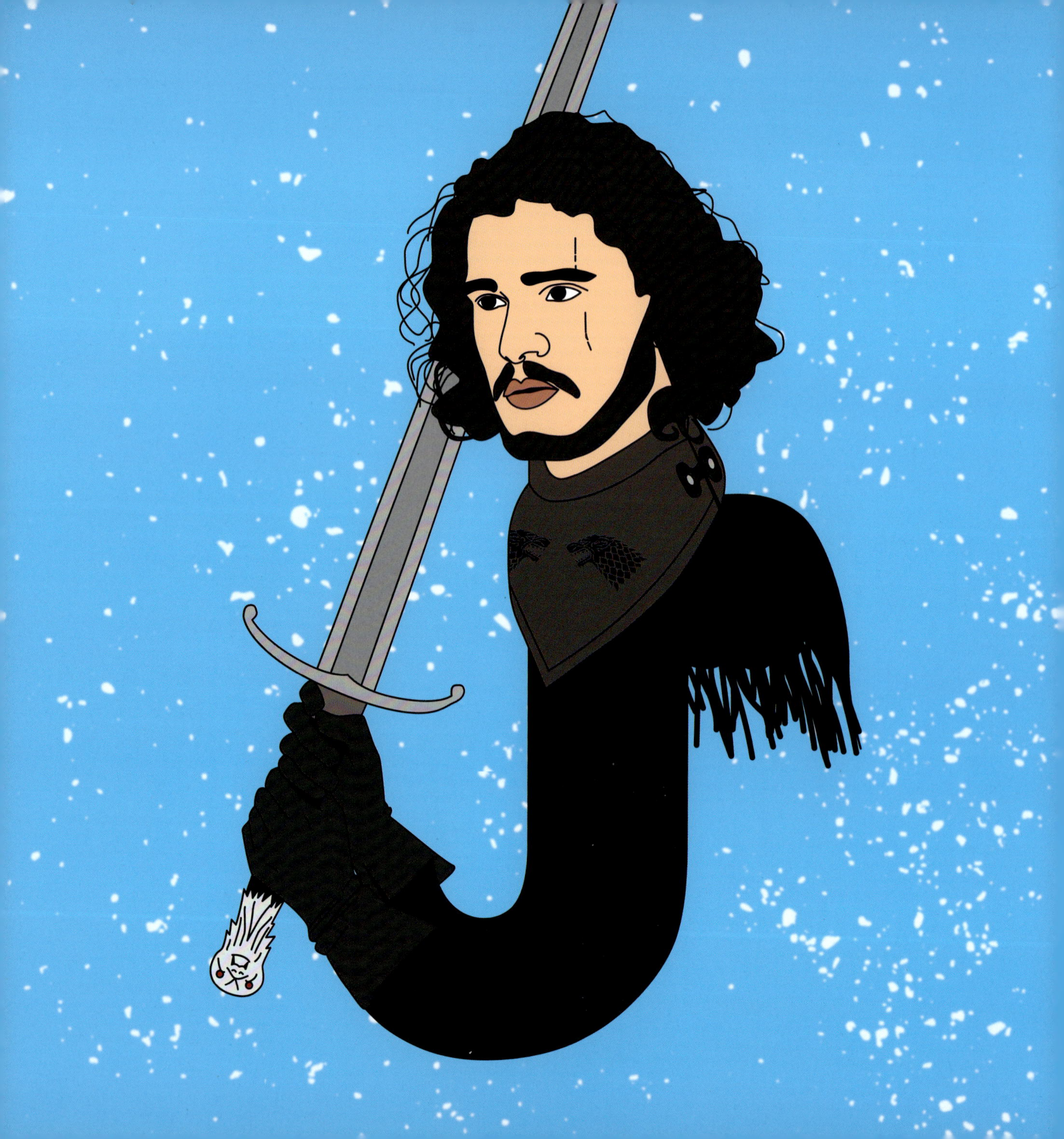

Jj

J is for Jon Snow.
Jon Snow went from the lesser child of Winterfell to the Prince that was Promised, from a man who knew nothing to the unifier of sworn enemies who helped save the realm. With direwolf Ghost and sword Longclaw at his side, not even death can stop this legendary leader.

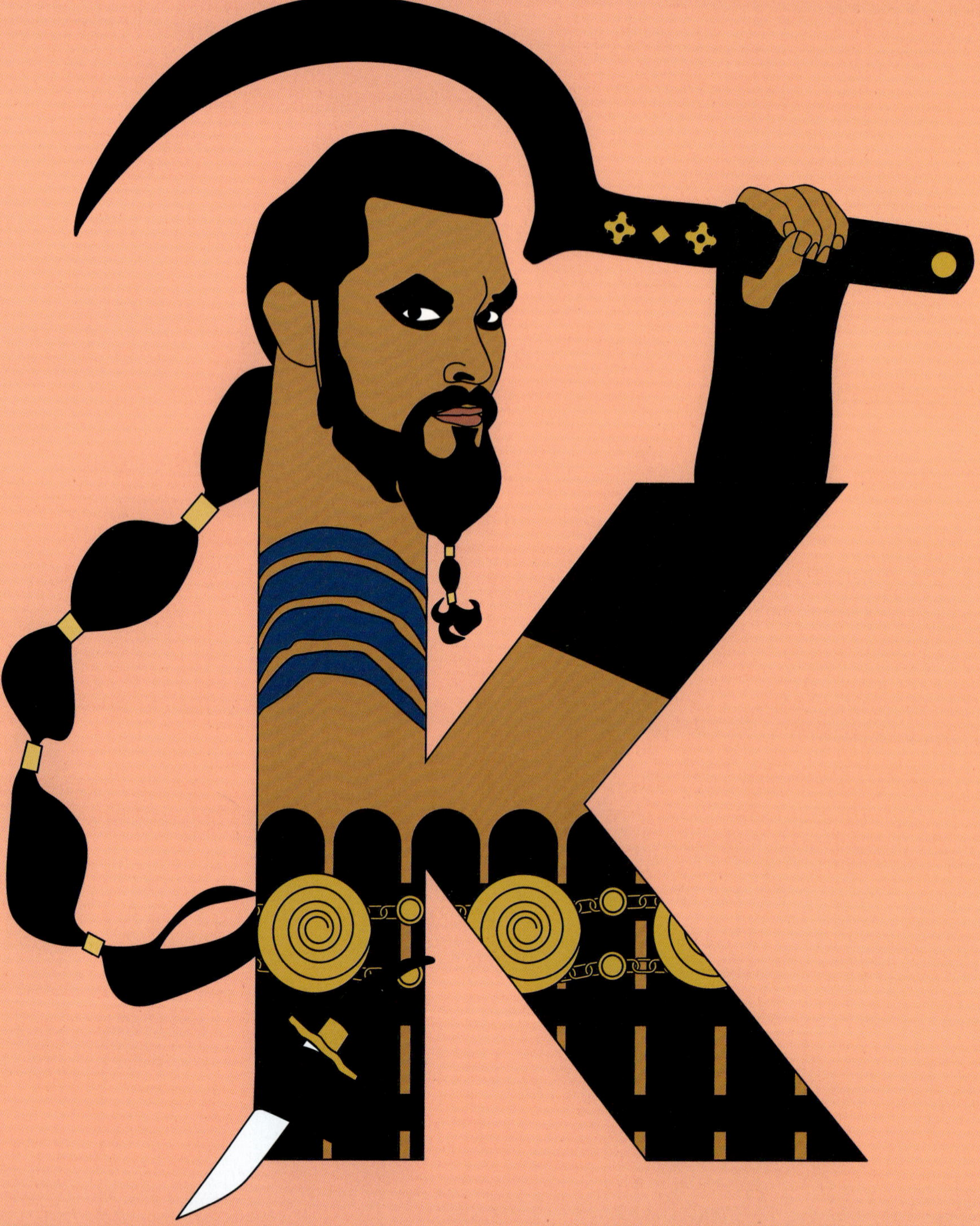

Kk

K is for **K**hal Drogo.
One look at this Dothraki's hair and it's clear that this warlord is not someone to mess with. A golden crown for Viserys and a gruesome end for the defiant Dothraki Mago are just two examples of Khal Drogo's legendary savagery.

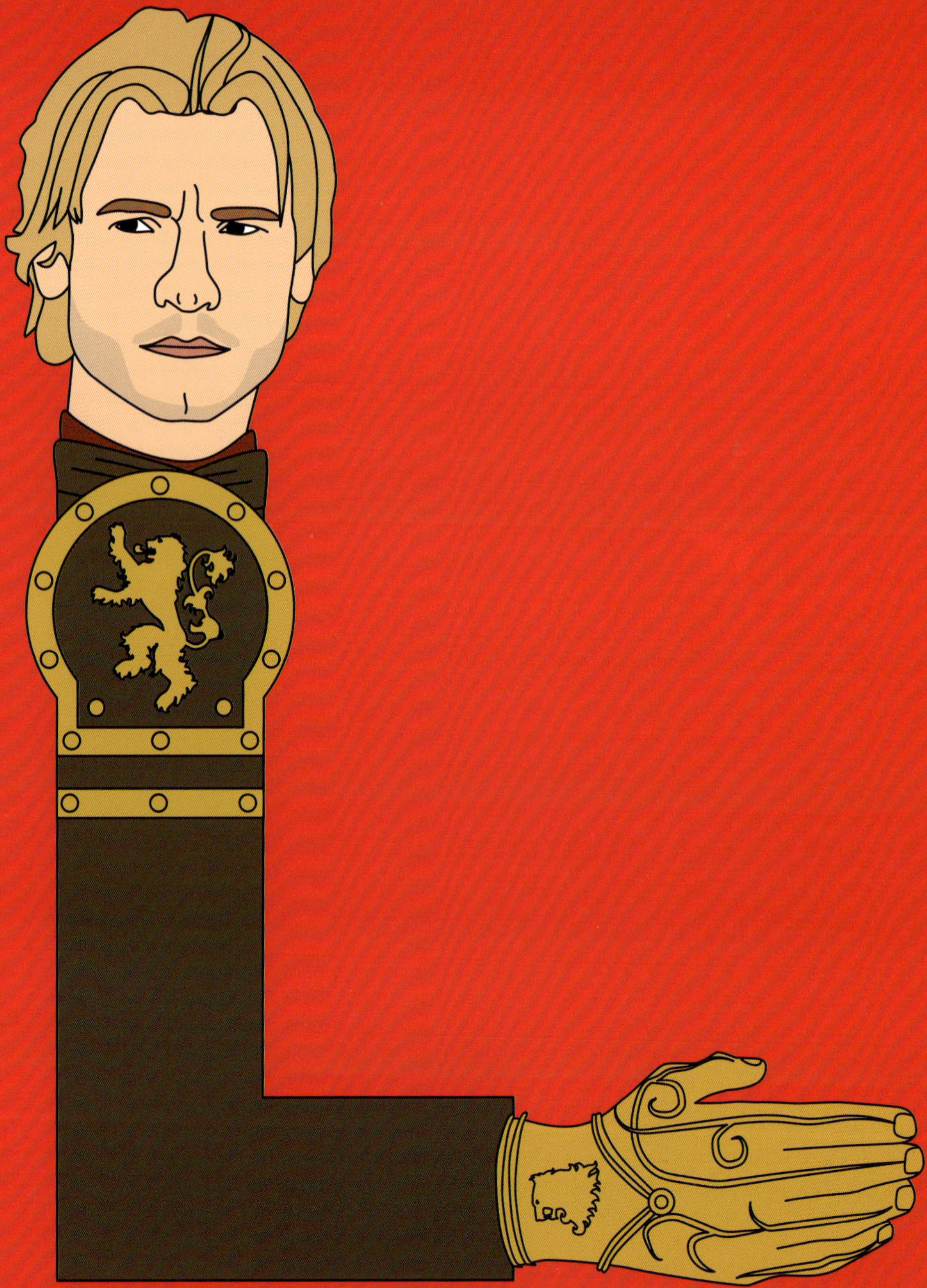

Ll

L is for Jaime Lannister. As the man with the golden hand who took down the Mad King, the 'Kingslayer' is known throughout the realm for his legendary ability to wield a sword. It's just too bad he can't fight those rumors about him and his twin sister Cersei.

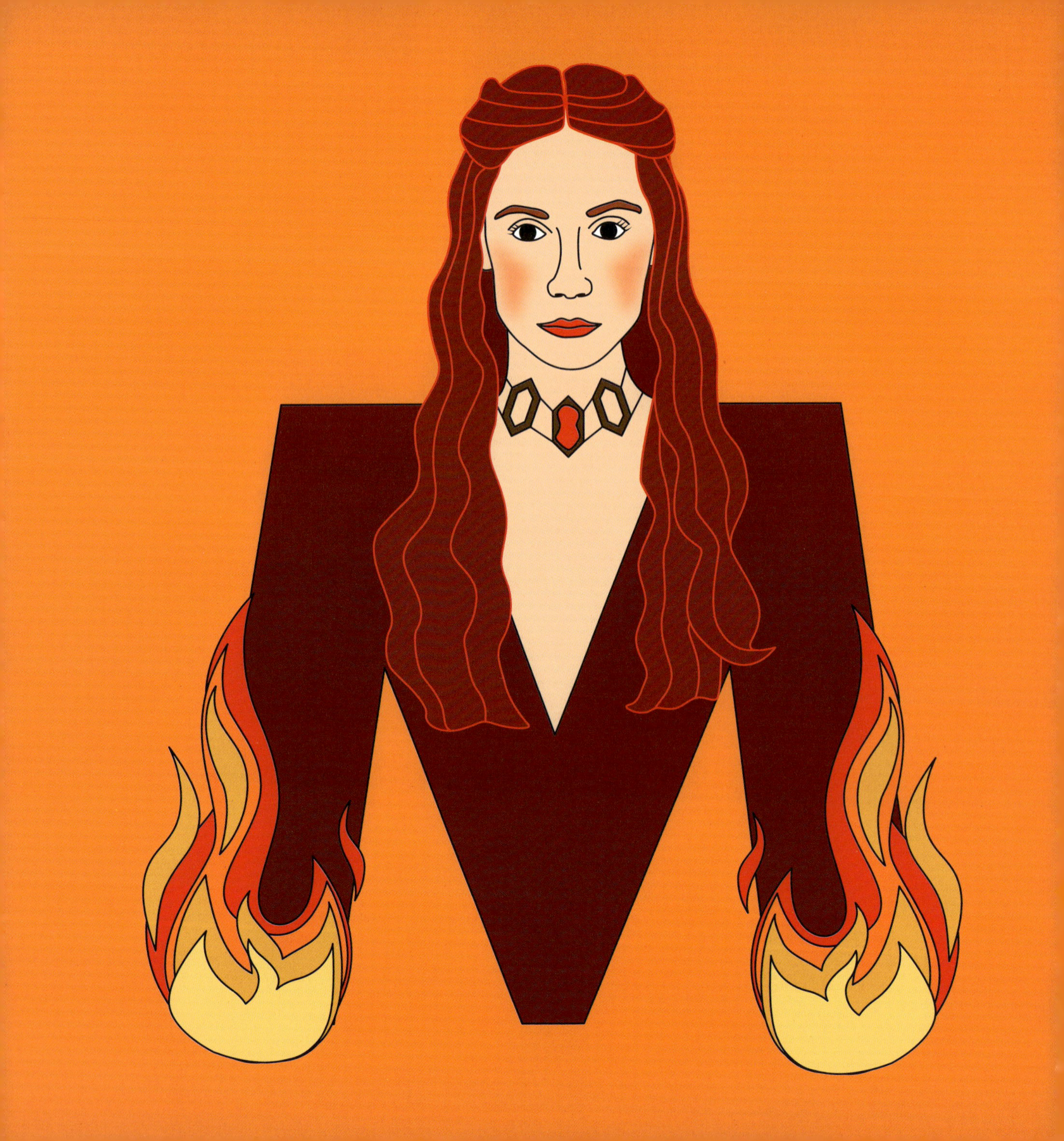

Mm

M is for **M**elisandre. This legend has a thing for the color red—and for some serious magic. Though many are skeptical of this priestess, it's Melisandre's mystical powers that revive Jon Snow, ignite the Dothraki against the White Walkers, and help inspire Arya to fulfill her ultimate destiny.

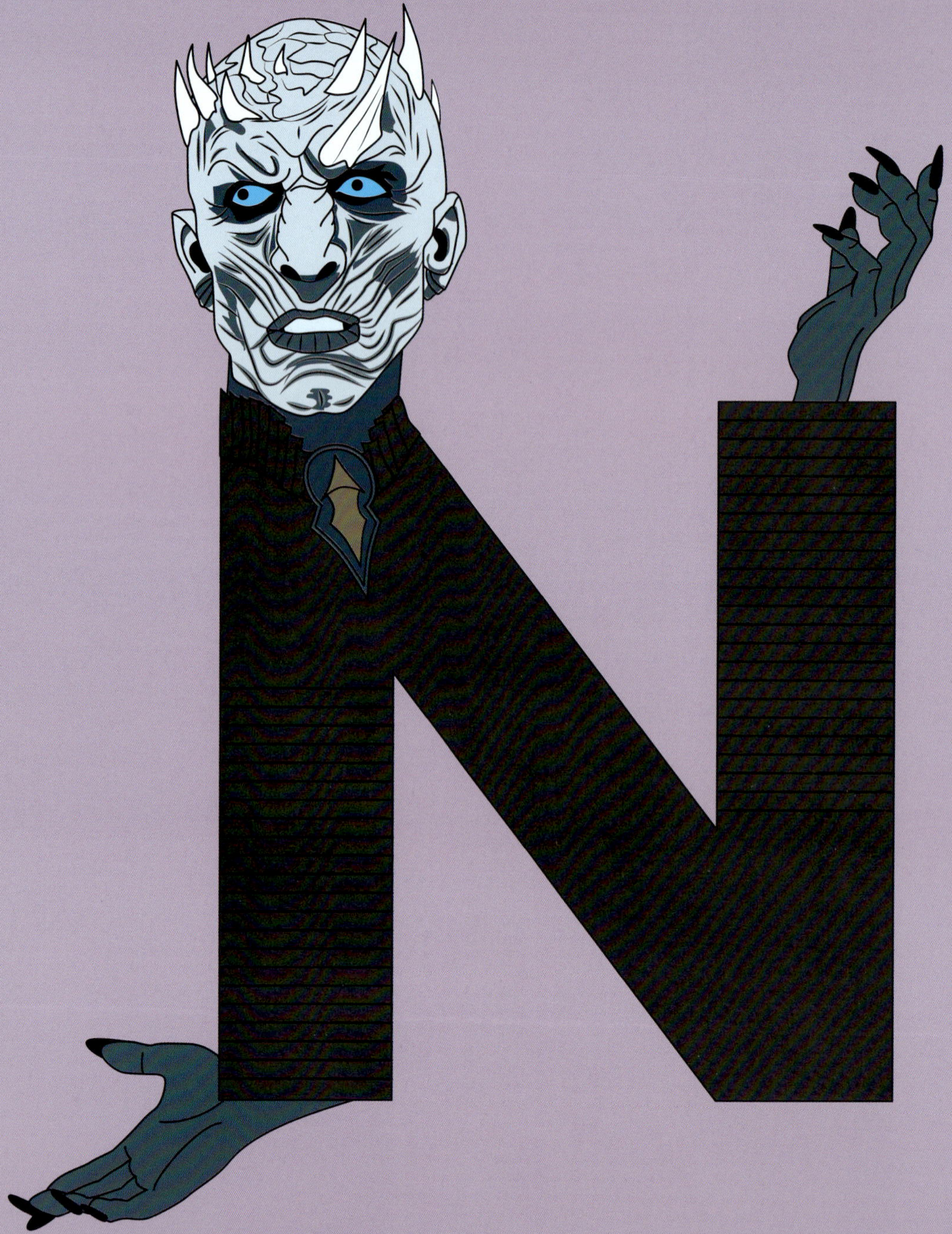

Nn

N is for the **N**ight King. This legend brings the storm. Winter is coming, and the Night King is leading the charge. With his army of White Walkers behind him, the Night King is ready for another Long Night to reign. Good thing Arya Stark has that Valyrian dagger of hers.

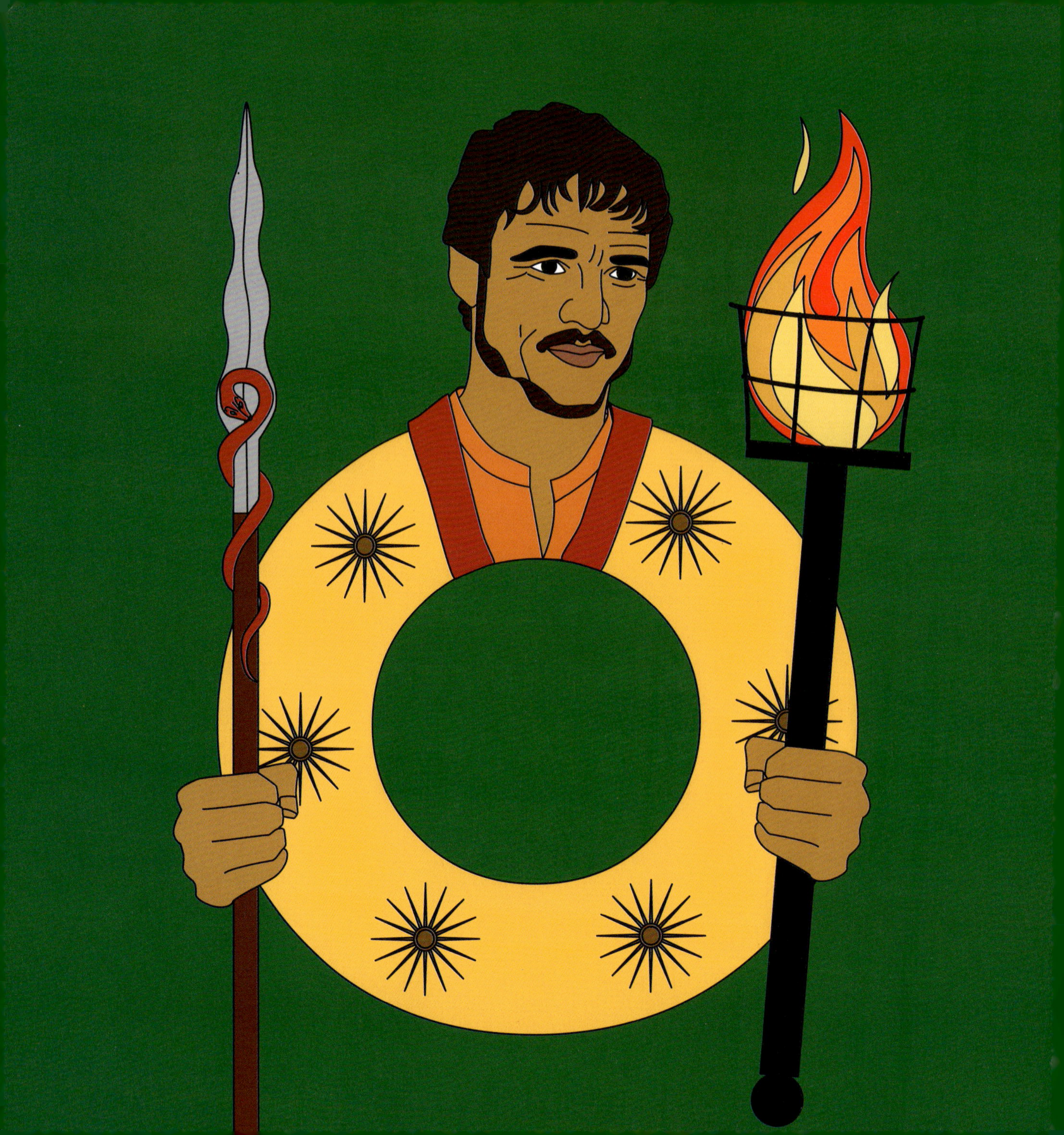

Oo

O is for **O**beryn Martell. The 'Red Viper of Dorne' is known for his legendary, stylish fighting tactics. With his signature staff, he can take on anybody, and he certainly knows how to celebrate. Oberyn just needs to do a better job of keeping his eyes on the prize in combat.

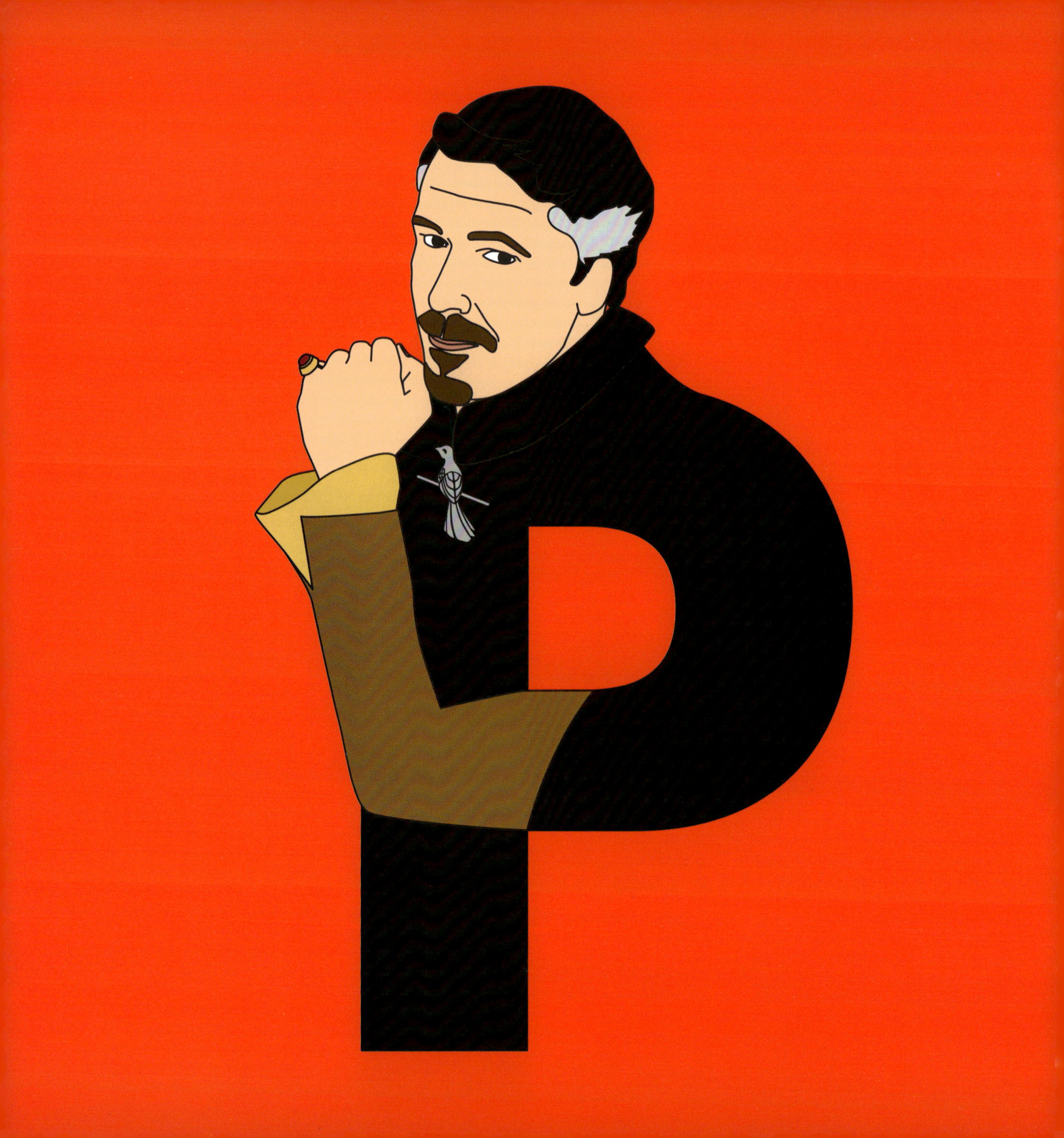

Pp

P is for **P**etyr Baelish. Chaos is a ladder, and this legendary manipulator does his best to climb it. 'Littlefinger' has his fingers in just about everything. But such a tangled web of double-crosses and lies can only lead to demise. Just ask the Stark sisters.

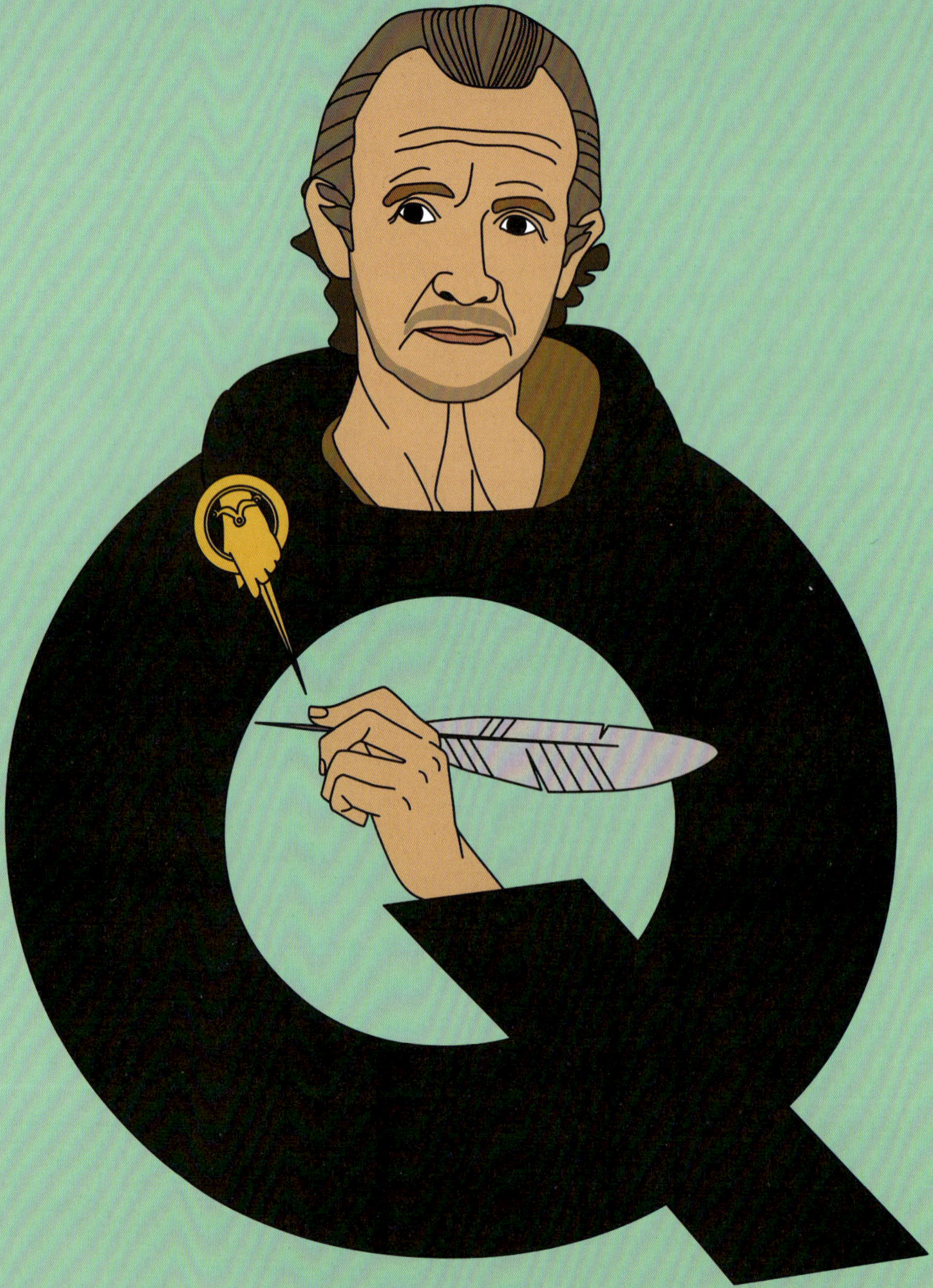

Qq

Q is for **Q**yburn.
This line-crossing maester was thrown out of the Citadel only to land on his feet as Cersei's Hand. It was Qyburn's handiwork that helped Jaime swing a sword again. But helping turn the 'Mountain' into a monster was this odd little legend's undoing.

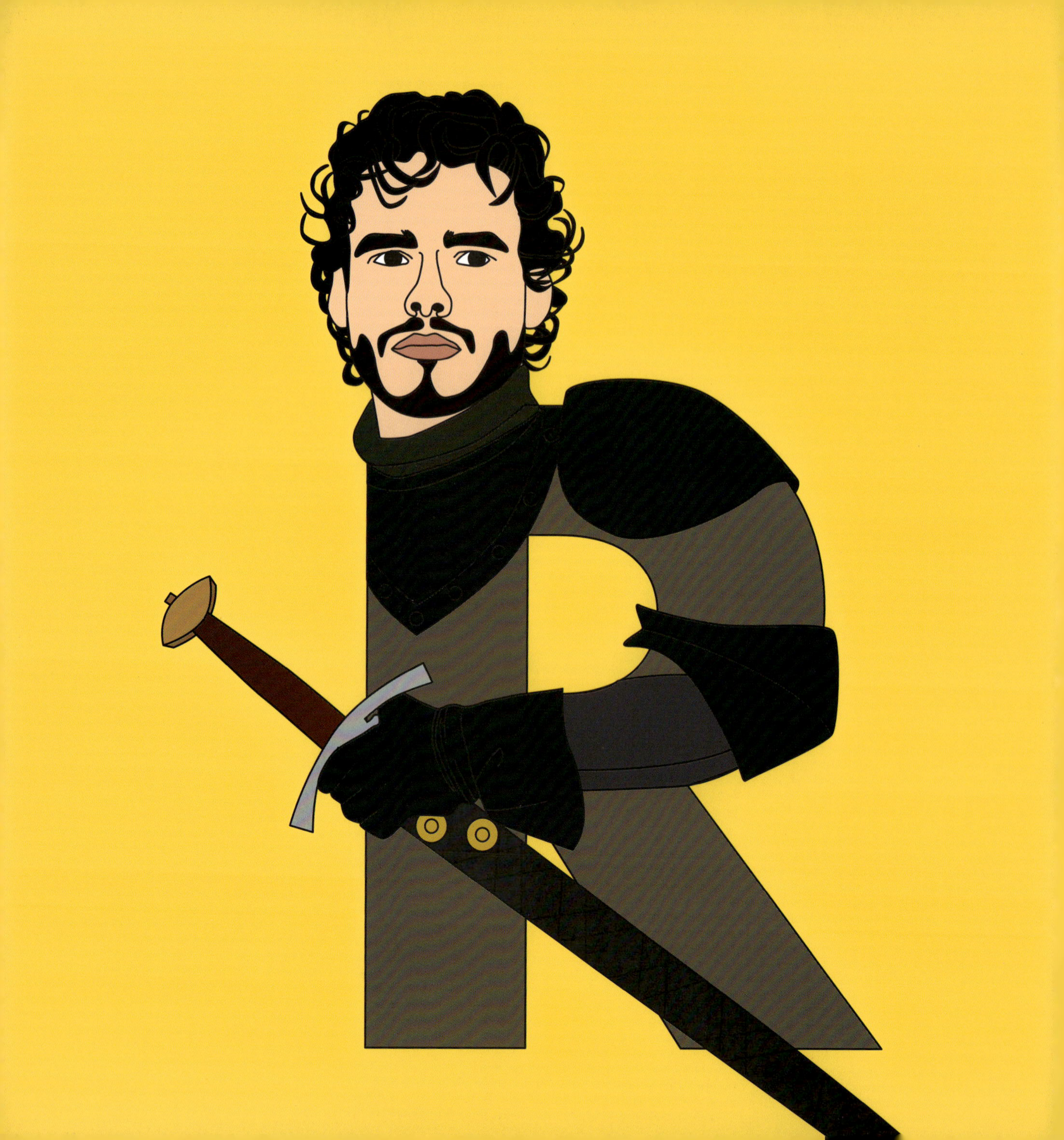

Rr

R is for **R**obb Stark. Don't go to a wedding with this guy. The legendary 'Young Wolf' follows in his father's noble footsteps as the King in the North. Things seem to be going well as Robb wins battle after battle. But then the Lannisters send their regards.

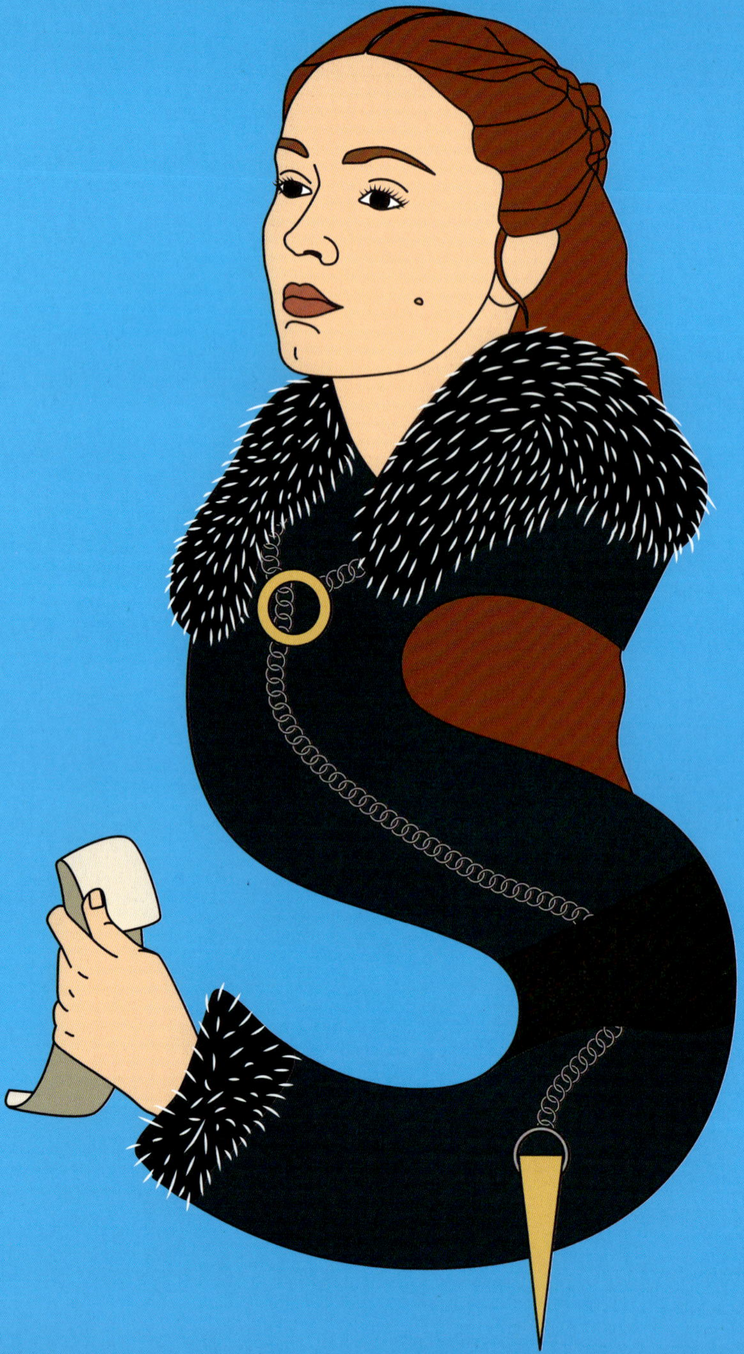

Ss

S is for **S**ansa Stark.
Many underestimated her.
Most of them are gone now.
Humiliation and abuse from
some of the vilest creatures
in Westeros can't keep this
legend down. With an
unbreakable spirit, Sansa
outlasts her awful husbands
to become Queen of the North.

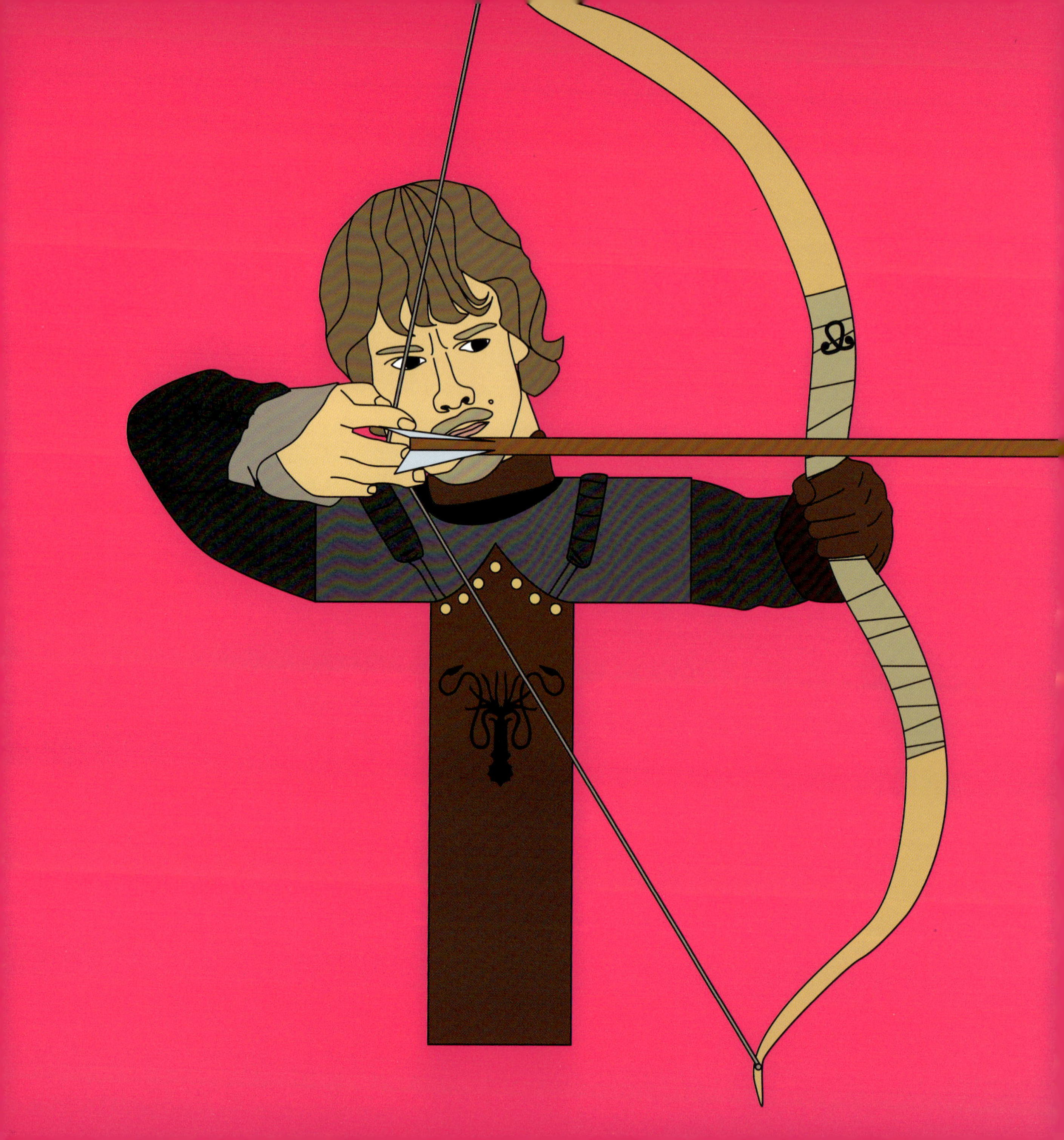

Tt

T is for Theon Greyjoy. Theon can never figure out exactly who he is. Is he a Greyjoy or a Stark? Is he Theon or Reek? This Ironborn legend may lose his pride at the hands of the merciless Ramsay Bolton, but there's no questioning his bravery when faced with sure death.

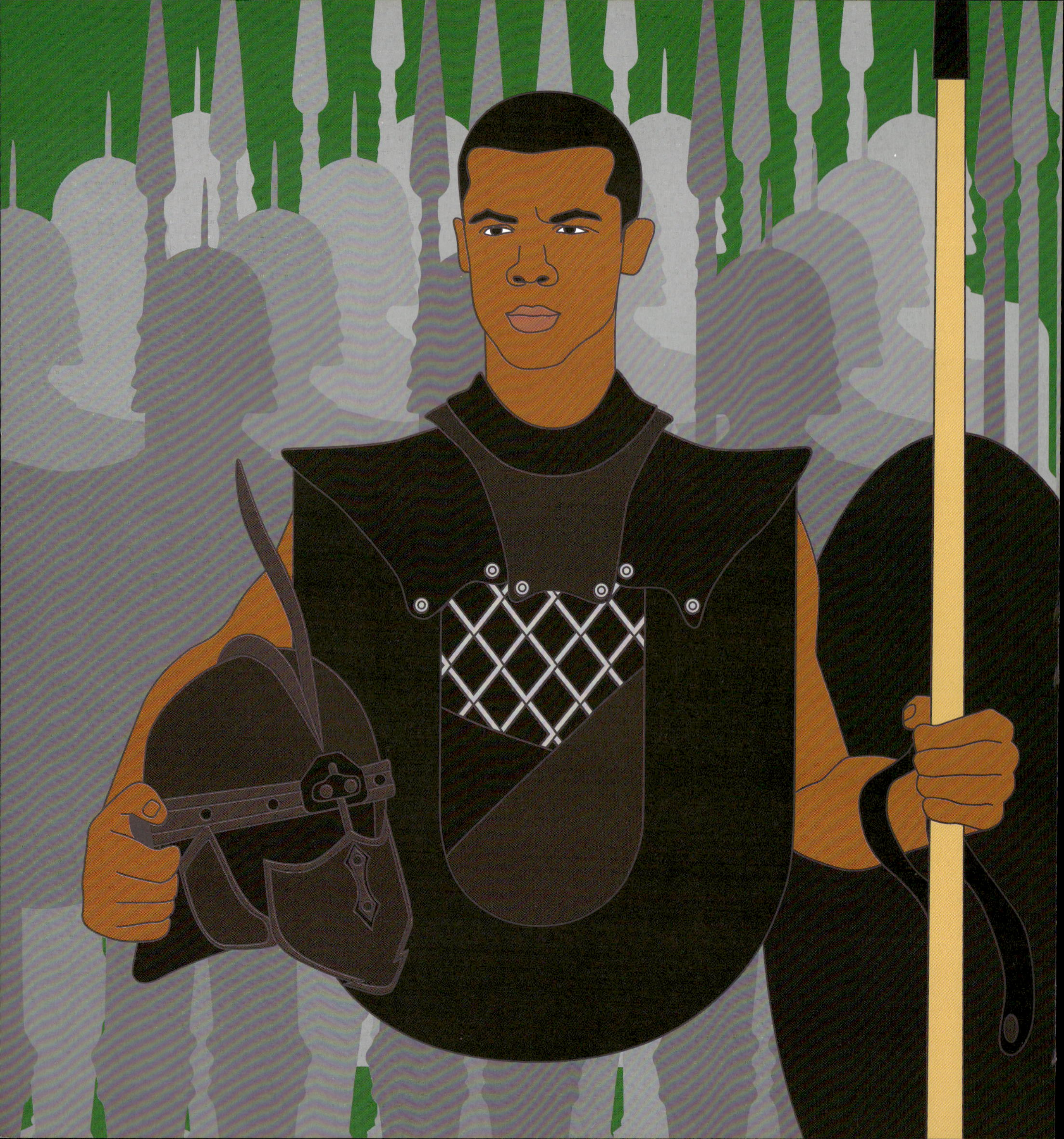

Uu

U is for the **U**nsullied. Thanks to their upbringing and training, these legends have only one thing on their mind. Originally slaves, the Unsullied were freed by Daenerys Targaryen. Now, led by Grey Worm, these warriors of few words but immense fighting skill dutifully follow Dany's orders without question.

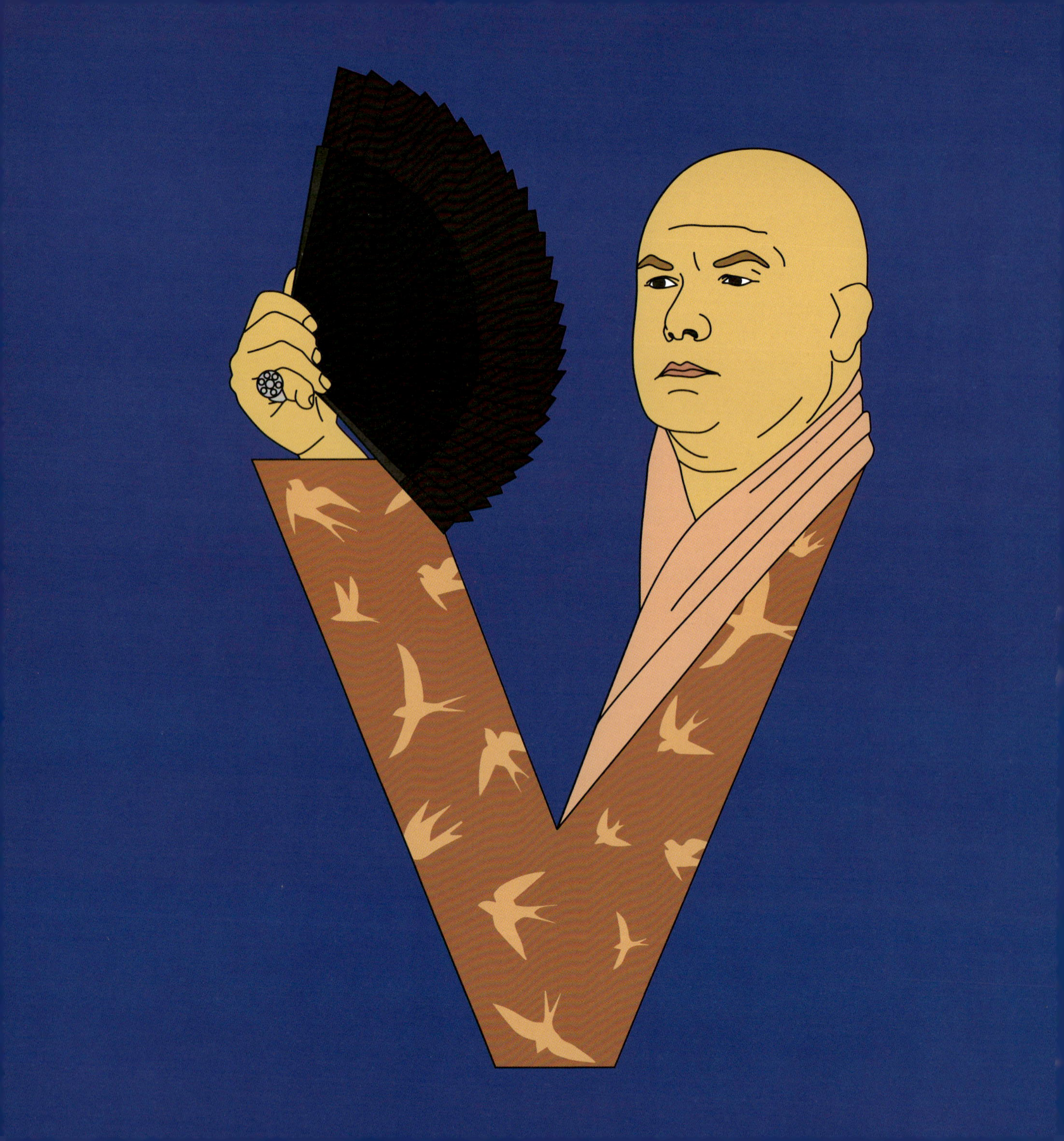

Vv

V is for Varys.
Don't get caught in the web of this 'Spider.' With his flock of little birds, this Master of Whispers seems to know just about everything. Loyal to the realm, Varys waters his weeds of influence from the Red Keep all the way across to the far side of the world.

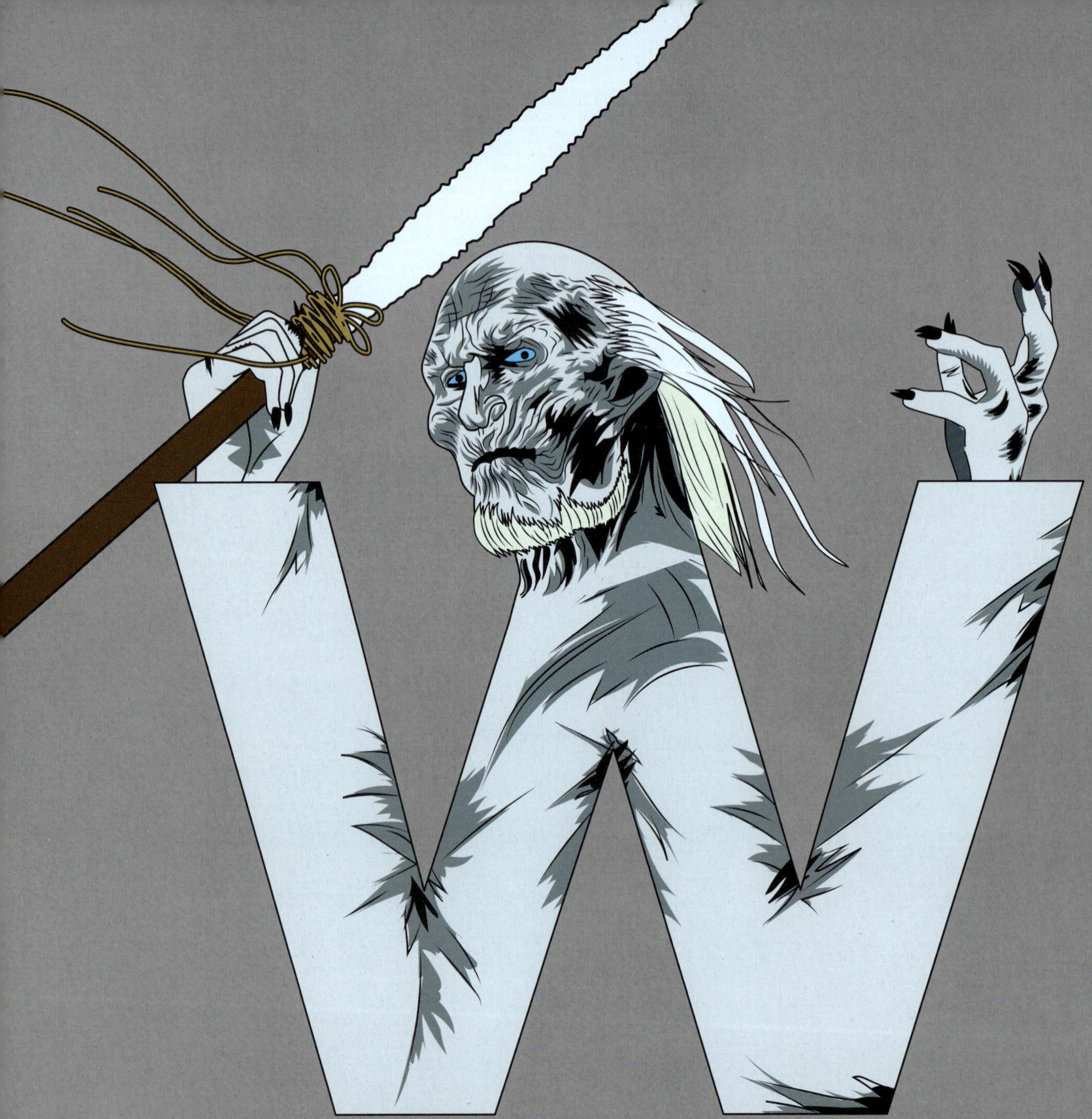
W

Ww

W is for **W**hite Walkers. This icy army of the undead mindlessly follows its leader, the Night King, on a mission to destroy every living thing. Always up for a Long Night, these monstrous legends can only be slowed by dragonglass and Valyrian steel.

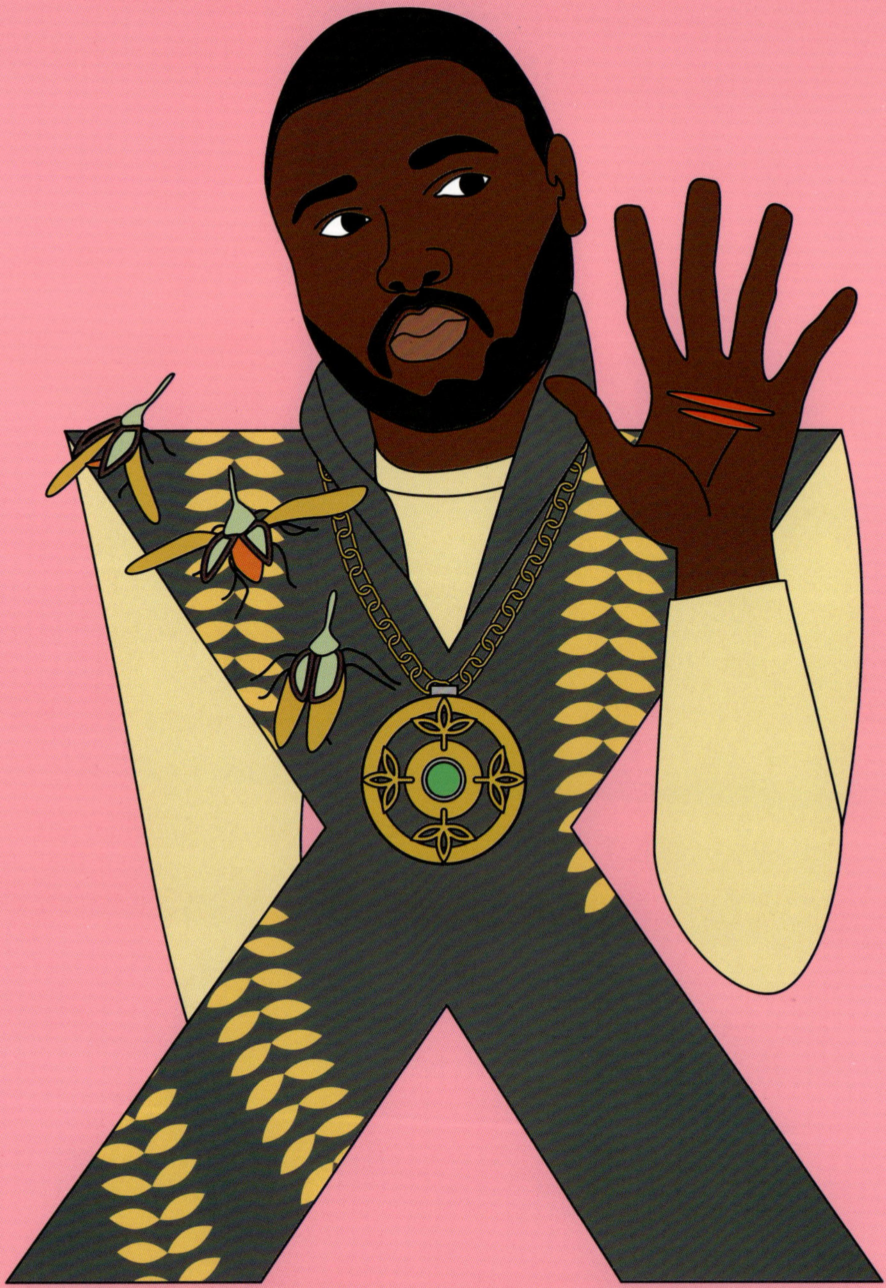

Xx

X is for **X**aro Xhoan Daxos. The self-proclaimed richest man in Qarth, merchant Xaro acts as the host with the most when Daenerys comes for a visit. But glittering gold can't cover up the fact this legendary liar's treasure vault is as empty as his morals.

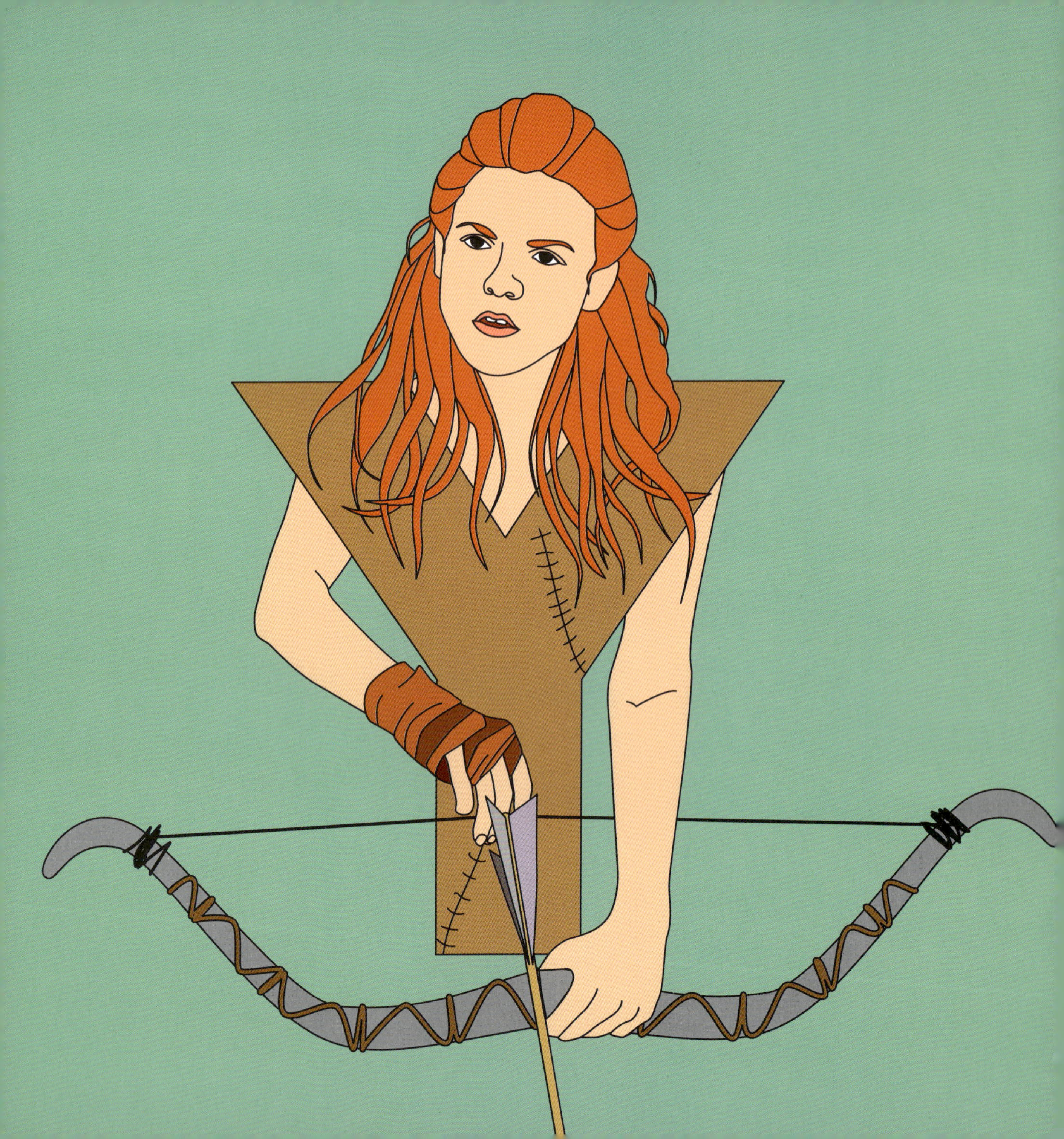

Yy

Y is for **Y**gritte.
This proud wildling archer's arrow hit Jon Snow straight in the heart, teaching him some of life's greatest lessons. A legend from north of the Wall, Ygritte is a skilled warrior, though the battle between her head and her own heart is a major issue.

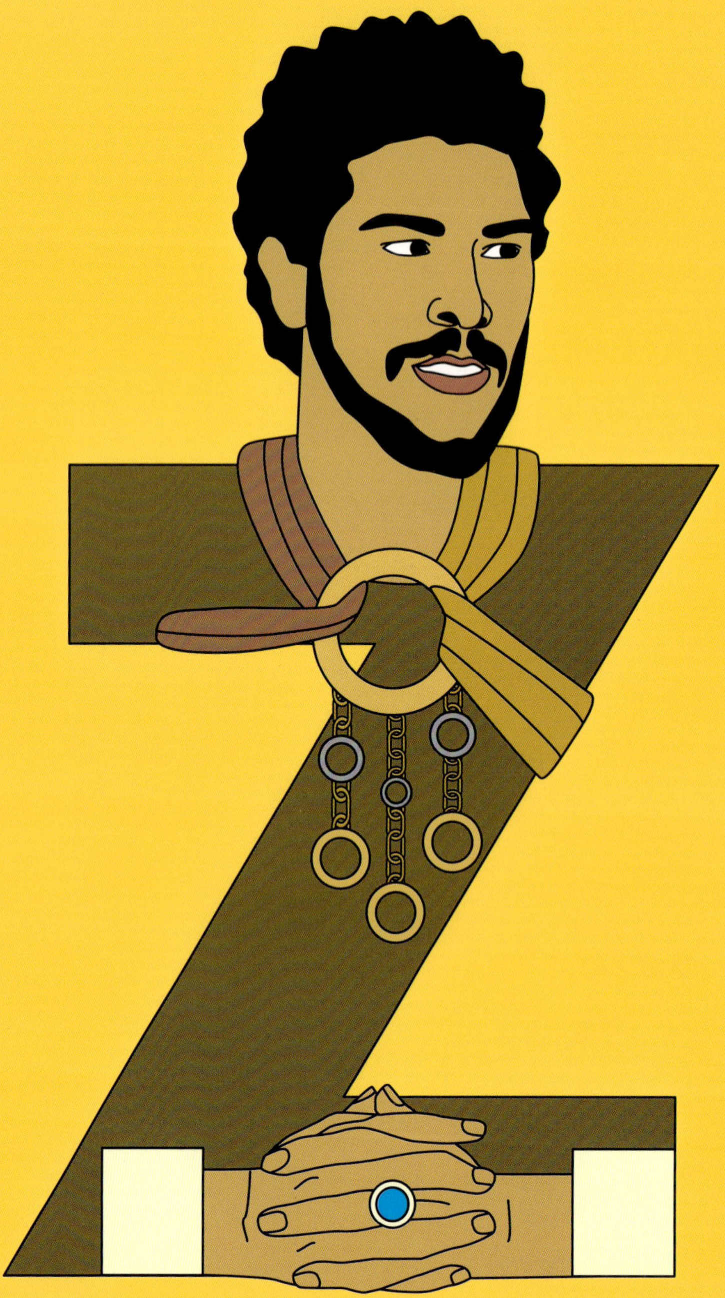

Zz

Z is for Hizdahr **z**o Loraq. From slave trader to Dany's almost-second husband, Hizdahr had his life forever changed when the Mother of Dragons arrived in Meereen. But his death ends up being an unintended consequence of Dany's attempt to free the people of Slaver's Bay.

The ever-expanding legendary library

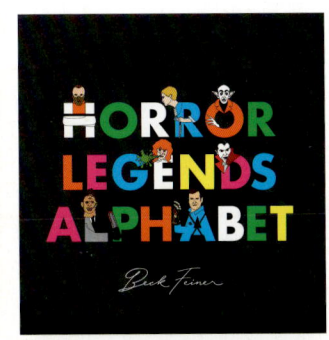

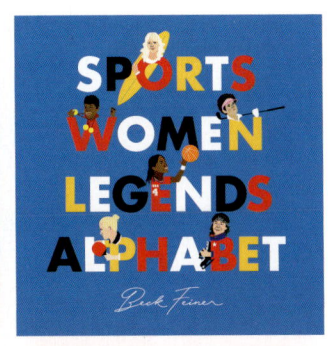

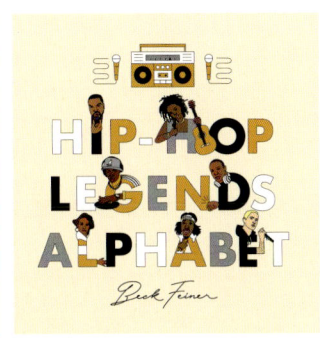

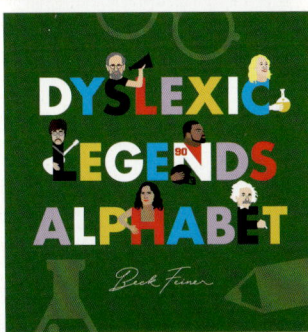

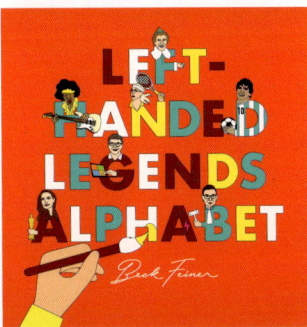

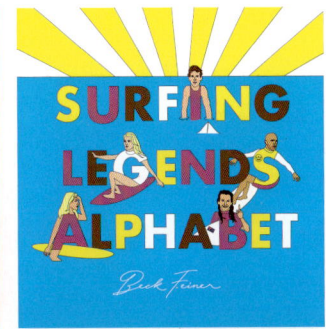

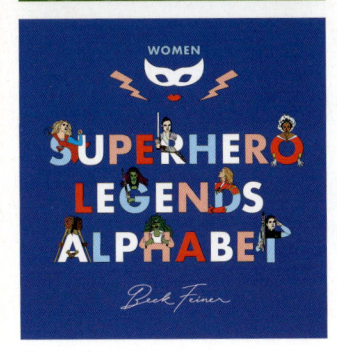

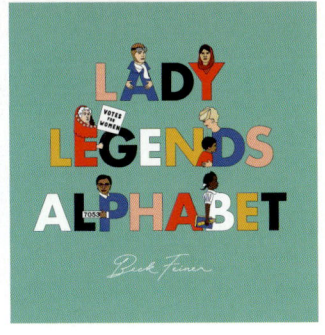

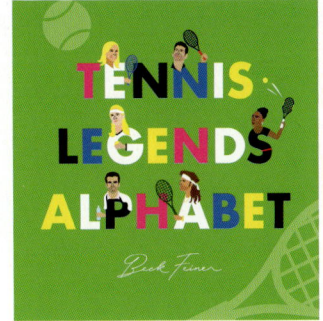

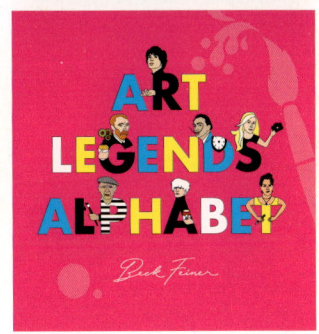

- HORROR LEGENDS ALPHABET
- SPORTS WOMEN LEGENDS ALPHABET
- HIP-HOP LEGENDS ALPHABET
- LAKERS LEGENDS ALPHABET
- DYSLEXIC LEGENDS ALPHABET
- LEFT-HANDED LEGENDS ALPHABET
- SURFING LEGENDS ALPHABET
- GUITAR LEGENDS ALPHABET
- SUPERHERO LEGENDS ALPHABET
- LADY LEGENDS ALPHABET
- TENNIS LEGENDS ALPHABET
- ART LEGENDS ALPHABET

EXPLORE THESE LEGENDARY ALPHABETS & MORE AT WWW.ALPHABETLEGENDS.COM

GOT LEGENDS ALPHABET
www.alphabetlegends.com

Published by Alphabet Legends Pty Ltd in 2022
Created by Beck Feiner
Copyright © Alphabet Legends Pty Ltd 2022

Printed and bound in China.

9780645200164

The right of Beck Feiner to be identified as the author and illustrator of this work has been asserted by her in accordance with the Copyright Amendment (Moral Rights) Act 2000.

This work is copyright. Apart from any use as permitted under the Copyright Act 1968, no part may be reproduced, copied, scanned, stored in a retrieval system, recorded or transmitted, in any form or by any means, without the prior permission of the publisher.

This book is not officially endorsed by the people and characters depicted.

ALPHABET LEGENDS